Marshmallow CLOUDS

written by LESLIE PARROTT

illustrated by TERRY TAYLOR

Zonderkidz

Zonder**kidz**™

The children's group of Zondervan

www.zonderkidz.com

Marshmallow Clouds
ISBN: 0-310-70349-2
Copyright © 2003 by Leslie Parrott
Illustrations copyright © 2003 by Terry Taylor

Requests for information should be addressed to:
Zonderkidz, Grand Rapids, Michigan 49530

Editor: Gwen Ellis
Art Direction & Design: Laura Maitner

Printed in China
03 04 05/HK/4 3 2 1

for
Jack and John
my sons
-Leslie Parrott

To Lynn and Clare with all my love.
Special thanks to my sister Kelly.
-Terry Taylor

Why did God make broccoli so yucky to eat?
And please don't tell me we've got liver for meat!
If I were in charge, I'd get rid of that stuff.
I'd put sugar in food, till it tastes good enough.

Peanut butter puddles would suit me just fine.
So would candy corn lampposts and licorice sunshine.

Or how 'bout trees made of leafy green taffy
And a peppermint pathway would make me quite happy.

I wonder why God didn't plan it that way?
He surely had something in mind...I'd say.

He didn't ask me, but I'd have made it known.
With chocolate seedlings a fine forest could've grown.

If flowers of bubble gum grew in the ground,

I'd water with gumdrops
all the year round.

Marshmallow clouds could float over my head,

And fill the plump pillow
that rests on my bed.

I'd make cucumbers from caramel—

that'd be pretty funny!

I'd give them all up for candy, you see.

If God would ask me, I'd have plenty of advice,
I'd substitute whip cream for spinach and ice cream for rice.

What a sugary world I'd make if I could,

The more I think, though, it really wouldn't be good.

Peanut butter puddles would be far too sticky.

God made them with raindrops so they wouldn't get icky.

As for giving up beans, carrots, lettuce...you know?
God knew we needed these for our bodies to grow.

My candy-coated world was a pretty silly thought,
Just think what would happen to a chocolate forest when hot.

I'm glad God's in charge of the world today.

I wouldn't change a thing—I like it this way.